Dear Parents and Educators,

Welcome to Penguin Young Readers! As parents and educators, you know that each child develops at his or her own pace—in terms of speech, critical thinking, and, of course, reading. Penguin Young Readers recognizes this fact. As a result, each Penguin Young Readers book is assigned a traditional easy-to-read level (1–4) as well as a Guided Reading Level (A–P). Both of these systems will help you choose the right book for your child. Please refer to the back of each book for specific leveling information. Penguin Young Readers features esteemed authors and illustrators, stories about favorite characters, fascinating nonfiction, and more!

Max & Ruby™: Ruby Scores a Goal

LEVEL 2
GUIDED READING LEVEL **G**

This book is perfect for a **Progressing Reader** who:
- can figure out unknown words by using picture and context clues;
- can recognize beginning, middle, and ending sounds;
- can make and confirm predictions about what will happen in the text; and
- can distinguish between fiction and nonfiction.

Here are some **activities** you can do during and after reading this book:
- Make Connections: Ruby has a hard time scoring a goal because she is distracted by her brother's noisy robots. Can you remember a time when you were distracted? Discuss what you did to get focused again.
- Compare/Contrast: In the beginning of the book, Ruby is angry at her brother for letting his robots get in the way of her soccer game. How does Ruby feel toward her brother at the end of the book?

Remember, sharing the love of reading with a child is the best gift you can give!

—Bonnie Bader, EdM
  Penguin Young Readers program

*Penguin Young Readers are leveled by independent reviewers applying the standards developed by Irene Fountas and Gay Su Pinnell in *Matching Books to Readers: Using Leveled Books in Guided Reading*, Heinemann, 1999.

Penguin Young Readers
Published by the Penguin Group
Penguin Group (USA) Inc., 375 Hudson Street, New York, New York 10014, USA
Penguin Group (Canada), 90 Eglinton Avenue East, Suite 700, Toronto, Ontario M4P 2Y3, Canada
(a division of Pearson Penguin Canada Inc.)
Penguin Books Ltd., 80 Strand, London WC2R 0RL, England
Penguin Group Ireland, 25 St. Stephen's Green, Dublin 2, Ireland
(a division of Penguin Books Ltd.)
Penguin Group (Australia), 250 Camberwell Road, Camberwell, Victoria 3124, Australia
(a division of Pearson Australia Group Pty. Ltd.)
Penguin Books India Pvt. Ltd., 11 Community Centre, Panchsheel Park, New Delhi—110 017, India
Penguin Group (NZ), 67 Apollo Drive, Rosedale, Auckland 0632, New Zealand
(a division of Pearson New Zealand Ltd.)
Penguin Books (South Africa) (Pty.) Ltd., 24 Sturdee Avenue,
Rosebank, Johannesburg 2196, South Africa

Penguin Books Ltd., Registered Offices: 80 Strand, London WC2R 0RL, England

Based upon the animated series *Max & Ruby*
A Nelvana Limited production © 2002–2003

Max & Ruby™ and © Rosemary Wells. Licensed by Nelvana Limited NELVANA™ Nelvana Limited.
CORUS™ Corus Entertainment Inc. All rights reserved. First published in 2009 by Grosset & Dunlap,
an imprint of Penguin Group (USA) Inc. Published in 2012 by Penguin Young Readers, an imprint of
Penguin Group (USA) Inc., 345 Hudson Street, New York, New York 10014. Manufactured in China.

Library of Congress Control Number: 2009009295

ISBN 978-0-448-45235-7   10 9 8 7 6 5 4 3 2 1

PENGUIN YOUNG READERS

LEVEL 2
PROGRESSING READER

Max & Ruby

Ruby Scores a Goal

7/12 $13.55 B+T

Penguin Young Readers
An Imprint of Penguin Group (USA) Inc.

Ruby, Roger, and Louise

are in the yard.

They are playing soccer.

Roger is the best goalie.

Max is Ruby's little brother.

He is in the yard, too.

He is playing with his robots.

The robots say,

"Alert! Alert!"

"Warning! Warning!"

"Danger! Danger!"

Louise kicks first.

Ruby cheers, "Give me an

L-O-U-I-S-E!

What does that spell?

LOUISE!"

Oh no!

Louise misses the goal.

Now it is Ruby's turn.

She will try to make a goal.

Then one robot shouts,

"Alert! Alert!"

The robot is very loud!

Ruby's kick goes wild.

Ruby is mad at Max.

"Max, your robot

made me miss the goal!

Roger is a great goalie.

I cannot score a goal

with all that noise."

Roger says,

"Try again, Ruby!"

Louise cheers for Ruby.

"Give me an R-U-B-Y!

What does that spell?

RUBY!"

"Ready! Set! Kick!"

says Ruby.

Oh no!

Look what is coming!

Ruby trips over the robot.

Her kick goes wild again.

Louise and Roger ask,

"Are you hurt?"

Ruby says,

"I am okay.

I will try one more time.

But first . . . "

Ruby goes over to Max.

"We cannot play

with your robots in the way.

Go play over there!"

Max puts his robots

in his wagon.

Then he pulls

the wagon away.

Oh no!

Two robots fall out

of the wagon.

They walk over to Ruby.

This time, Ruby hears

the robots.

She moves left.

She moves right.

The robots do not trip her.

Whap!

Ruby kicks the ball.

Oh no!

Look what is coming!

One robot says,

"Danger! Danger!"

Roger looks around.

"What? Who is that?"

He does not watch the goal.

Whoosh!

Louise cheers for Ruby.

"Ruby scored a goal!"

Roger cheers for Ruby.

"You did it!"

Ruby is happy.

She says, "I did it!

But I had help."

Ruby gives a big cheer.

"Give me an R-O-B-O-T!

What does that spell?"

"Robot!" says Max.